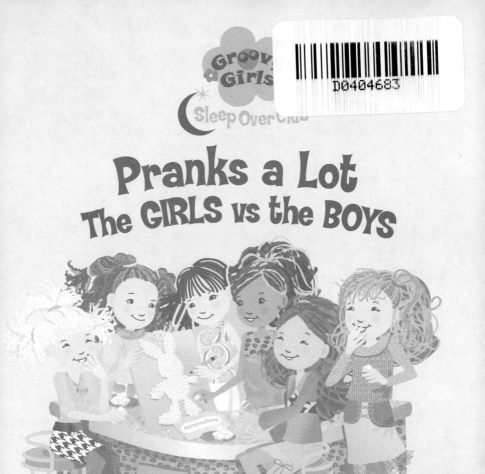

Groovy Girls
Sleep Over Club

Pranks a Lot
The GIRLS vs the BOYS

Robin Epstein

Scholastic Inc.
New York Toronto London Auckland Sydney
Mexico City New Delhi Hong Kong Buenos Aires

To David J,
Think of this as your applause break

Cover illustration by Taia Morley
Interior illustrations by Bill Alger, Yancey Labat, and Steven Lee Stinnett

ISBN 0-439-65790-3

12 11 10 9 8 7 6 5 4 3 2 1   4 5 6 7 8 9/0
Printed in the U.S.A.
First Scholastic printing, October 2004

How to Build a Bunny
the Groovy Girls way

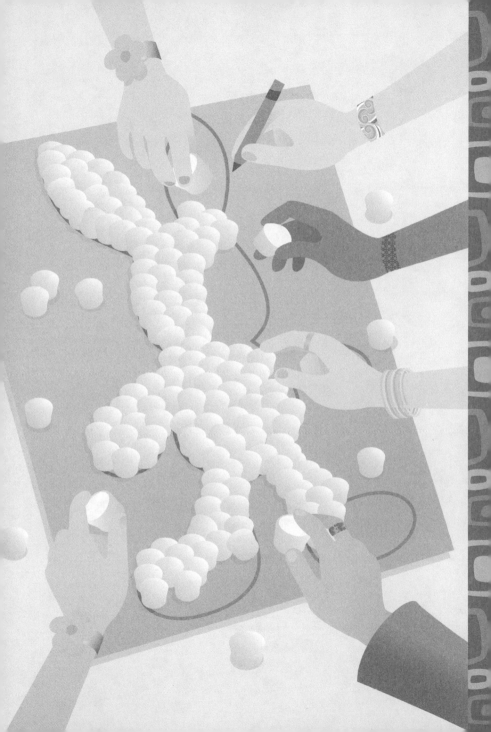

Chapter 1

Take Note

Dear Oki,
The last Groovy Girls sleepover was so supreme, Reese and I want to have another one...
In fact, howze 'bout Sat. night? You free?
Party #2 = 2X the fun!

Chow,
O'Ryan

Dear O'Ryan,
Purr-fect! Love the idea. And I just got glammie new jammies to wear! Can't wait for Groovy Girls Slumber Party No. 2 on Saturday night.
Stay Groovy!
SWAK,
Oki

Dear Oki,

P.S. Wonder if I'll get to see Mike napping on the couch again like I did last time. He looked soooo cute...even if he couldn't stay up all night!

O'Ryan

O'Ryan smiled as she reread her note. She'd written it while Mrs. Pearlman was correcting the class's spelling exam.

Whoever did best on the test would go on to the school-wide spelling bee. So Mrs. P. was concentrating hard as she made big red X's through misspelled words (or "*mispelled*" as Gwen misspelled it).

O'Ryan knew it'd be the perfect time to pass the note.

So she folded the message and nodded at Oki. Then, she tossed it.

And that's when the unthinkable happened...

Interception!

Mike, the great goalie on O'Ryan's soccer team—and the VERY boy she'd just written about (who thought she was a pretty pizzazzy player herself)—snatched  the note from the air.

He grabbed it like a ball heading for the net!

O'Ryan's eyes bugged.

Oki clapped her hand over her mouth.

This was a *deeeeeee-zaster.*

"Spam!" O'Ryan said. If Mike read that note, it would be the most embarrassing—most horrible—most *ugh*-producing moment EVER!

Mike held the note in his right hand and glanced between Oki and O'Ryan. Then he tossed the note up in the air and caught it in his left hand.

He looked at the girls again and smiled.

He hadn't opened the note yet. He just kept tossing it back and forth—teasing them.

Hand to hand. Right to left. Left to right.

I need to get that note back, O'Ryan thought to herself. But from playing on the same soccer team as Mike, she knew he could react fast. She also knew her desk was too far away from his to grab the note back that quickly.

But Oki wasn't worried about desk distance or reaction time. She just wanted that note! After all, it was meant for *her*, not Mike! So when he tossed it in the air again, Oki jumped for it.

Unfortunately, time and distance *did* matter.

And by the time Oki was mid-air, Mike had already recaptured it.

Worse, as Oki leaped up, her chair leg scraped the floor. It made enough noise for their teacher to hear.

Mrs. Pearlman turned around.

The *first* thing she saw was Oki looking guilty.

The *second* thing she saw was O'Ryan staring in disbelief.

And the *third* thing she saw was Mike reading what looked like a little note.

Mike now knew:

1. The girls had caught him sleeping during their first Groovy Girls sleepover on Saturday— *after* they'd made a bet about who could stay awake the latest.

And

2. That O'Ryan thought he looked cute while catnapping.

"Mike," Mrs. Pearlman said. "You weren't just passing a note, were you?"

Hearing Mike's name, Reese turned around. Somehow she *just knew* her twin sister, O'Ryan, was involved in some way.

Gwen thought just the idea of Mike passing notes was funny.

Oki bit her lip and squinched her eyes shut.

But it was O'Ryan's face that told the story.

And told it in bright colors!

Her face had turned as red as a rose.

Mike was silent for a second. Which felt

more like an hour. Then he shook his head. "No, Mrs. P.," he said, "*I* wasn't passing a note. I swear."

Mrs. Pearlman eyed Mike carefully. She wanted to see if her stare would crack him. But Mike stayed solid, sticking to his story.

After all, he *was* telling the truth.

He hadn't *passed* a note.

He'd only *caught* one.

"Well," Mrs. Pearlman replied, "then I suppose no notes were passed." She looked at Oki and O'Ryan again. "Unless anyone *else* would like to clear the air?"

Oki and O'Ryan sat still as stones—they were practically rock candy.

But Mrs. P. was onto them.

"Oki," she said. "Anything I should know?"

Mrs. P. was good at getting answers. But no way was Oki going to fall for her tricks...*this* time.

"Oh, everything's *mar-vy*, Mrs. P. I'm just a little zonked," Oki said, trying to change the subject. "We had a no-sleep sleepover on Saturday night."

"A no-sleep sleepover?" Mrs. Pearlman asked. "What's that?"

"It's where you stay up all night, if you can... but we couldn't," Gwen said, chiming in softly.

But it was just loud enough for Mike to hear.

"Well, if it's *just* that you're tired, take a few deep breaths," Mrs. P. said. "You know, get some air going to the noggin. And then let's continue on with our spelling prep."

As the other students reached into their desks for their spelling books, Oki looked to O'Ryan. She flashed her best friend the thumbs-up sign. And O'Ryan nodded, feeling relieved, too.

Well at *least* they were able to distract Mrs. P.

And Mike *hadn't* turned their note over to the teach.

After all, he could have said, "Nope, I wasn't passing a note. *BUT* O'Ryan and Oki were. And here it is!"

He could have gotten them into BIG trouble.

But he didn't. Chose not to.

Just decided to keep their note private.

Even though he had *read* it.

O'Ryan looked over to Mike, and he smiled.

But Mike's wasn't a smile that totally said, "Glad to help!" or "I'm your new best buddy."

No.

Not quite.

It was more a smile that seemed to spell T-R-O-U-B-L-E.

Chapter 2

Something Old, Something New

"Reese, it looks like you're wearing Grandma's underpants!" O'Ryan said that afternoon after school. Reese had just tried on a pair of long khaki shorts at their mother's store, "Hey, Betty."

"Well, it looks like a rainbow B-U-R-P-E-D on your back!" Reese replied as O'Ryan modeled a tie-dyed T-shirt.

Hey, Betty was a vintage clothing shop. Since being "vintage" meant the clothes were old, whenever the girls were at the store, they got to see all the old-fashioned old fashions.

And they got to go through all the boxes for their mom—which was like a treasure hunt, since you never knew what you'd find. Besides clothes, other old stuff sometimes turned up, too. Like metal lunch boxes with old TV shows pictured on them. And lava lamps, skateboards...even pet rocks!

O'Ryan was especially enjoying being at the store that afternoon because it was taking her mind off some more *recent* history: the Mike note-grabbing-and-reading-interception incident at school that day. In her whole life, O'Ryan had never remembered being so embarrassed, or turning so red!

Helping their mom at the store made the twins feel important, too. Especially when customers asked for their assistance. They'd answer questions like:

"Where are the dressing rooms?"

"Is everything in this bin really $1?"

"Do you think these pants make my backside look big?"

That October day, as the twins went through the boxes, they were also scouting for ideas for Halloween.

If O'Ryan wore the tie-dyed T-shirt she had on, she decided she could be a hippie chick. All she'd need to add were granny glasses and love beads!

Reese hadn't found anything that tickled her yet—except for a hot-pink feather boa. But then, in one of the boxes, she saw something glimmer...

"Hey!" she yelled excitedly. "Check it O-U-T!" Reese pulled a red-sequined beret from the box and put it on her head.

"Looks like you're wearing a mirrored shower-cap," O'Ryan replied.

Reese looked at herself in the mirror and started laughing. That was *exactly* what it looked like.

"When was it in style to wear *that*, Mom?" O'Ryan asked.

"Well, never, really." Mom laughed.

"Too F-U-N-N-Y!" Reese said.

"What's with the spelling, sweetie?"

"It's B-E-E season, Mom," Reese answered.

"We took the test for the school-wide spelling bee today," O'Ryan explained. "I thought it was kind of T-U-F-F."

"That's no shockeroo." Reese smiled, "'Cause that test was T-O-U-G-H. *Not* T-U-F-F."

O'Ryan blew her sister the raspberry, then went back to the boxes. "Funky!" she said, holding up a pair of rainbow-colored socks with spaces for each toe. "It's, like, for someone with monkey feet."

"Hey!" Reese cried, when she got to the bottom of one of the boxes. "I think there's some sort of game down here." She held it up and showed it to her mother.

"That's a Ouija board," Mom replied.

"A *wha-cha* board?" O'Ryan asked.

"It's spelled O-U-I-J-A, but it's pronounced *WEE-jee*," Mom explained. "It was one of my favorite games when I was your age."

"Really?" Reese asked.

"You mean you were actually *our age* once?" O'Ryan said.

"Yeah," Reese said, giggling. "In *vintage* times."

"F-U-N-N-Y!" Mom replied.

"I've never seen a game like this before," O'Ryan said. "First of all, there's no place to put batteries!"

"And second of all," Reese added, "there's no starting point."

"Which brings us to point number three," O'Ryan continued. "There's no finish line, either!"

The board had the letters of the alphabet on it, and the numbers 1, 2, 3, 4, 5, 6, 7, 8, 9, 0. The words "yes," "no," and "good bye" were printed on it, too. And in its box, the girls found a cream-colored, heart-shaped plastic thing-y with a round see-through glass in the middle.

"What is *this*?" O'Ryan asked, pulling out the plastic piece.

"That's the pointer," Mom replied, placing it on the board and sliding it back and forth.

"*Bee-zarr-o*!" Reese exclaimed. "How do you play?"

"Yeah, what's it all about?" O'Ryan asked.

"Well, the game is sort of about telling you your past, present, and future," Mom answered.

"*Whoa.* It tells fortunes?" Reese said, throwing up her hands. "Like it can tell if you guys will ever let me get a dog?"

"That's the idea," Mom replied. "But I might be able to tell you the answer to *that* one just as easily!"

"You're not saying someone knows my *future*, are you?" O'Ryan asked. "Who is this Ouija guy, anyway?"

"This is so supreme!" Reese said excitedly. "I can't wait to ask it what I'm gonna get for my birthday. I wanna play right now!"

O'Ryan, however, got very quiet.

Reese looked at her twin and saw a little twitch in her eye.

She knew that twitch.

It was a twitch that meant Y-I-K-E-S!

"Someone's a fraidy-cat!" Reese teased.

"Am not," O'Ryan replied, turning away.

O'Ryan wasn't going to admit being frightened

of anything—even of a Ouija dude that might know her future.

Even if maybe she *was*.

A little.

"Anyway, at least *this* someone isn't scared of harmless little bugs like someone *else* someone knows!" O'Ryan added quickly.

Reese couldn't deny that bugs freaked her out.

Because *yuck*!

They totally did!

"Well, sure," Reese replied, "but it's completely normal to be bugged by bugs 'cause they're creepy. They're crawly. *And* they're gross. But being jumpy about a board game is just *ba-nanas*!"

"I'm telling you, I'm not scared of some silly, dumb, crazy-lazy board game. That's totally *ree-dic*!" O'Ryan insisted. "And to prove it, I think we should play the game at our sleepover on Saturday night."

"Great," Reese said.

"Great," O'Ryan replied.

So *that* was *that*!

O'Ryan felt pretty proud of herself for *squashing* the fraidy-factor on that one. Plus, with the other Groovy Girls by her side, she was sure she wasn't going to let anything *bug* her!

Gather 'Round, Girls!

"Okay, first thing you want to do," Mom said, explaining the directions of the game, "is place the pointer in the center of the board. Then, lightly rest two of your fingers on top."

"Why?" asked Reese.

"Because that'll help the Ouija board feel connected to you," Mom said.

Once Mom and the girls placed the pointer on the center of the Ouija board and each put two fingers on top of it, Mom continued: "Good. Now you can ask the Ouija any questions you want."

"Like what?" Reese asked.

"You can try asking it about the future," Mom replied. "Or about the past. And you'll see, once the question has been put out there, the pointer is going to start moving to give you a response."

"And what will it say?" O'Ryan wondered.

"It might say, 'Yes.' It might say, 'No.' And it might give you a number, if you ask it something mathematical. *Or*, if the Ouija is so moved," Mom said with a smile, "it might even spell out its response. *But*, that's just between the Ouija and Y-O-U!"

Chapter 3

Practice Makes
P-E-R-F-E-C-T

"It's not gonna work," Oki said, leaning over the
Ouija board at the slumber party on Saturday night.
"How can a Ouija man know our beeswax?"

Since discovering the Ouija board, the twins
could talk about nothing else. And *that's* how all
the Groovies came to be playing it at their
sleepover.

They couldn't even wait until Gwen—or, as they called her, the *"Latest* Greatest Gwen"— arrived, late (as usual).

"She can jump in whenever she gets here," Vanessa said. "Let's start!"

"You'll see, Oki," said Reese, taking the pointer out of the box. "The Ouija will start working as soon as we set the mood."

It was already dark outside, and the fireplace in the living room was glowing, so the mood *seemed* pretty set to O'Ryan already. But...

"Make it darker!" Vanessa said, pointing to Yvette. "Shut the lights and show me some spirit!"

Whereas Oki didn't believe in the power of the Ouija board, Vanessa totally did. In fact, it made perfect sense to her that some sort of Ouija dude out there knew the score. As a natural leader herself—captain of her soccer team and future member of the Supreme Court—*this* was something she could relate to.

"I hope it can tell me what I'm going to look like when I grow up!" Reese said excitedly.

"If you're lucky, you'll start looking more like me," O'Ryan replied, smiling at her twin.

"O'Ryan, we already *know* the board doesn't give scary fortunes," Reese said back, with a laugh.

"Let's start by giving it an easy question to warm up," Vanessa said.

The girls leaned in, and each of them pressed two fingers on the pointer.

"Oh, Mr. Ouija!" Yvette said, in a dreamy and dramatic voice. As an aspiring actress, Yvette really liked to get into any role she played. "On this day, ten days before Halloween—

and right in the middle of spelling bee season— can you tell us how many Groovy Girls there are?"

The girls looked down at the pointer.

They pressed their fingers against it more firmly.

And as each girl pressed, something amazing happened!

The pointer started sliding across the board!

It was slightly jerky at first—more like a skid than a slide—but soon enough, the pointer was in motion!!!

"*Huuuuuh,*" Yvette uttered, drawing in her breath.

The pointer slid over to the numbers at the

bottom of the board, moving past 1, 2, 3, 4, and 5. And it looked like it would keep sliding right past six.

But as fast as it started moving, it stopped!

"It stopped on six!" Reese said.

"Way to go, Weej!" Vanessa shouted.

"Wait a sec," Oki said, shaking her head. "There are only *five* of us here!"

"But it must *know* there are six of us."

And then right on cue, the doorbell chimed. *Ding dong.*

Reese opened the front door and in tumbled the "Latest Greatest Gwen."

"*There's* number six!" Vanessa replied to Oki.

"I know I'm late," Gwen said. "But the traffic was just awful!"

"What traffic?" O'Ryan asked. "You only live a couple blocks away."

"Yeah, but there was a traffic jam right in front of your house. See, my mom couldn't drive like her regular speedy self 'cause we got stuck behind Jay's mom's car. And she moves in slo-mo, as if no one's in a hurry behind her!"

"Jay from class?" Oki asked.

"Yup," Gwen nodded.

"Where was he going?" Yvette asked.

"Directly across the street!" Gwen replied.

"Jay was going to Mike's house?" O'Ryan asked.

"You betcha. And he was carrying a sleeping bag and pillow, too."

"Aw, isn't that cute?" Vanessa added. "The boys want to have a sleepover just like ours!"

"Wonder what boys do at a pajama party," Yvette said.

"Probably same as us—paint their nails, braid their hair, and give each other facials!" O'Ryan replied, and all the girls laughed.

"Well, no matter how good the cucumber facial, their slumber party won't be nearly as *beautilicious* as ours," said Vanessa.

"And certainly not as *dee-licious*," Gwen said, holding up a shopping bag. "'Cause, look! I brought marshmallows, graham crackers, and two bars of chocolate so we can make s'mores!"

"Yay," Reese replied, hugging her best friend. "I adore s'mores!"

"Me, too—three, four, and five!" Gwen said excitedly. "Should we make 'em now?"

"No, not yet," Vanessa replied. "We were just playing with the Ouija board, and we're going back to it."

"Oh," Gwen said, plopping down next to Reese. "Okay, but soon, right?"

"We'll see," Vanessa answered. "I mean, we all ate dinner before we came, right?"

The girls nodded.

"Well, without dessert, does it really *count* as a meal?" Gwen asked.

"Nice try, Gwen," Vanessa said, "but no cigar. Let's get back to the game."

The girls had just put their fingers back on the plastic pointer when the phone started ringing.

"I'll get it," Reese said, picking up. "Hello?"

"Yes, hello. I'm calling from A-One Telemarketing, and we're doing a survey."

"Maaaaaa!" Reese yelled. "Telephone!"

"Uh, no! Wait!" the caller said.

Suddenly, Reese clued in to the voice. It sounded an awful lot like a voice she knew. So she motioned to her friends to gather around the phone. Then she pointed to the caller ID screen on the receiver and nodded.

WELLSTONE, ANDREW, the phone screen read. Mike's father's name.

That "A-One Telemarketer" lived directly across the street and, not only that, the girls knew he had his best friend with him.

So now the Groovies knew what boys did at sleepovers:

They made phony phone calls to girls!

"I can't believe they're trying to prank us," Oki whispered.

"Well, they can *try* to prank us, but we're not going to let that happen, right, girls?" Vanessa whispered back. "Keep talking, Reese, and don't let on that we know it's Mike. Try to turn the tables on him."

Reese nodded. "Okay, Mr. Marketer. Now about your survey…you wanted to ask me some questions?"

"Ah, yes," Mike-the-Marketer replied. "A-hem, as I was saying." It sounded like he was trying to deepen his voice to sound like a TV announcer. "Have you and your friends ever wished you'd been able to stay up all night, but not been able to do it? If so, I've got just the product for you!"

"Okay," Reese replied. "Whatcha got?"

"It's top secret, so you need to listen very carefully, okay?"

"Uh-huh," Reese said. She motioned for the Groovy Girls to lean in closer so they could all hear better what Mike was going to say.

"You're *really* listening, right?" Mike asked.

"Yes!" Reese answered, and the girls leaned in closer still.

HOOOOOOONNNNNNNNNKKKKKKK!!

The earsplitting sound of an air horn ripped through the phone. The horn was so loud, it practically blasted the girls off their feet!

The next thing the girls heard was Mike and Jay laughing in the background. Then the boys hung up the phone.

Even though the Groovy Girls *knew* they were being pranked—and had fully expected to beat the boys at their own game—they still got punked!

This was unacceptable!

This demanded action!

Good news was, there were six Groovy Girls against two silly boys. So any way you divided it, the girls were three times as smart, three times as sharp, and three times as spunky as the two boys.

And if this was how the boys wanted to play, the Groovy Girls would play right back!

Chapter 4

Some Bunny's Gonna Get It!

"**Y**ou're kidding! Mike sleeps with a stuffed white bunny?" Vanessa asked.

The girls laughed as they tried to imagine it: Mike curled up with a fuzzy, furry toy rabbit!

O'Ryan hadn't previously told the Groovies that she'd seen Mike asleep with a stuffed animal when she had spied on him during their first slumber party.

But now that Mike had blasted them with the air horn, O'Ryan thought she had no choice but to spill his secret.

"This is incredible info," Yvette said. "Very juicy stuff."

"So juicy, it's practically freshly squeezed!" Reese added.

"And extra pulpy!" Gwen said. "But how do we use it so we don't lose it, you know what I mean?"

"Well, my older sister told me sometimes high school football teams steal each other's mascots," Vanessa replied. "So," she said, "maybe we should try to take his *wascally wabbit*!"

"We can't do that!" Oki replied. "That's too mean."

"Yeah, if we took Mike's rabbit, he'd probably be *hopping* mad!" Gwen said with a giggle.

"Well," O'Ryan added, "from being on his soccer team, I know he's kind of proud. So he'd probably be upset if he even *knew* we knew about his stuffed animal."

"Maybe we should just call him and tell him we've seen the bunny and are going to tell the whole class about it," Reese suggested.

"No," Vanessa said. "We need to be more creative than that."

"Yeah, we've got to do something dazzling," Yvette replied. "Something that shows our razzmatazz!"

"Ooh! I have an idea!" Gwen shouted. All the girls turned to her, hoping she had the perfect plan. "Let's make s'mores," she said, holding up her shopping bag and pulling out the marshmallows. "I am sooooo hungry!"

"*Gwen*!" Vanessa replied, rolling her eyes. "First we deal with the Mike situation. *Then* we make s'mores."

"Fine," Gwen said, hugging the bag of marshmallows to her chest, even though she didn't really think it was fine at all.

"Wait, that's it!" Oki cried, staring at the marshmallows. "We can show Mike we know he sleeps with a stuffed animal by making a marshmallow bunny!"

"Um," O'Ryan said, "explain, please!"

"Bunnies are fluffy, and marshmallows are puffy, right?" Oki replied excitedly. "So we make the bunny out of marshmallow puffs. Then we leave it for Mike on his doorstep. When he finds it, he'll be sooooooo embarrassed. It's a *no-brainer*, right?"

"It's supreme!" Gwen replied.

All the Groovy Girls were in total agreement.

One fluffy marshmallowy bunny coming right up!

"Grab some poster board, glue, and markers, girls," Vanessa instructed. "Then, let's bust open that marshmallow bag and let the fluff fly!"

As the most artistic in the group, Oki sketched the outline of a rabbit on the poster board. Then, the girls took turns gluing marshmallows to the drawing. They had just enough puffs to fill in the whole bunny. And Vanessa used the last one to stick on the cottontail.

"We need to add some sort of message to go with it," Yvette said when the picture was finished.

"Maybe we could come up with names we

think Mike could call his rabbit," O'Ryan suggested. "In case it doesn't have a name already."

"Yeah," Reese said. "Let's come up with a list."

So the girls started to brainstorm.

"I'd call the rabbit 'Ears,'" Reese said.

"How 'bout 'Honey Bunny'?" Vanessa suggested.

"What about '*Bug-zy*'?" O'Ryan replied, smiling slyly at Reese.

"I'll go with that one," Oki said about her BFF's choice.

"I like 'Carrot Cake,'" yelled Gwen. Then she shook her head. "See? I told you. I can't get my mind off dessert!"

"Ooh, I might name it 'Hare-y Potter,'" said Yvette.

If Mike already had a name for his bunny, the girls were sure their ideas were more clever.

So after they decided on the final list, Vanessa handed Reese the marker. "Here," she said. "You have the best handwriting, so write the choices next to the bunny."

When Reese finished writing "Top Five Names for Mike's Pretty Baby Bunny, by the Groovy Girls," the glue had dried on the marshmallows, and the girls were good to go!

Vanessa carried the poster board, and the Groovies followed her across the street to Mike's house. They carefully set the marshmallow bunny down on the welcome mat.

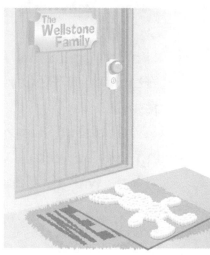

"Okay, ready, ladies?" Vanessa asked. "On the count of three, get ready to run!" She put her finger next to the doorbell. "One... two..." Then she pushed the buzzer and RANG THAT BELL. "Three!"

The Groovy Girls turned and ran back to the McCloud's, dashing behind the big bush in the front yard. And when they peeked out from it, this is what they saw:

Mike and Jay opening the front door and bending down to examine the girls' art project. Even from all the way across the street, they could see how much Mike was admiring their work!

Not.

At.

All!

"I think I can see steam coming out of his ears," Gwen whispered.

"Yeah," Reese said, "I bet he's turning as red as O'Ryan sometimes does!"

"We got him good," Yvette exclaimed, when the boys stomped back inside. "Great work, girls!"

The Groovies shook their right hands in the air, wiggled their butts, and turned around in a circle. This was their Groovy Girl victory dance.

"Now that that's taken care of—" Vanessa started to say.

"S'mores?" Gwen asked.

"No, not yet, Gwen. Let's get back to that Ouija board first."

So the girls went back inside and sat down around the board again.

It was even darker outside now than it was when the girls had first started playing the game. But instead of this making O'Ryan feel more afraid, now—especially after their successful prank—she wasn't going to let anything scare her. In fact, she was feeling very much in control of things!

"Okay," Gwen said. "Let's give it another try. Ouija board, I lost my hair band earlier. Where is it?" she asked.

The girls leaned in, and the pointer started moving.

P-O-C-K-E-T it spelled out.

Good speller!

"Pocket? That can't be right," Gwen said, reaching into the sides of her cargo pants. She turned the pockets inside out. Nothing.

The Ouija appeared to be wrong.

"Check *all* the pockets," Reese suggested.

Gwen reached into the pocket by her knee. "Whoa!" she shouted, pulling out a pink ponytail holder. "Impressive!"

"Are you kidding?" Oki asked. "You lose ponytail holders in your pockets all the time, Gwen. Everyone knows that! This board doesn't know *anything*...and I'll prove it."

"How are you going to do that?" Yvette asked.

"I'll show you," Oki replied. "Okay, Ouija, if you think you're so smart, what's the name of my cat?"

The girls were *spellbound* as they watched the pointer start to move again.

Well, *most* of the girls were spellbound.

O'Ryan was no longer scared of it—or impressed by it, either. Instead, she was simply amused by the fact that she was guiding the pointer—pushing it where she wanted it to go. And she was pretty sure the other girls hadn't figured this out yet.

The pointer first stopped on the letter **M**.

Then it traveled backwards across the board and paused on the letter **E**.

It slid forward and landed on the letter **O**.

And finally, it came to rest on the letter **W**.

MEOW?

"Wow, the Ouija board got it W-R-O-N-G," Reese said. "'Cause we all know your cat's name is Nyan, Oki."

Oki didn't say anything...but she didn't seem happy that she'd proven the board wrong.

"Oki," Vanessa asked, "what's the matter?"

"The word *Nyan* means meow in Japanese!" Oki replied softly.

"Holy guacamole!" Gwen said, totally amazed. "So not only does this Ouija board know what it's talking about, it even speaks a foreign language!"

The girls were so stunned by this (everyone except O'Ryan), that, when all of a sudden they heard spooky noises and saw two monsters in the window, their mouths dropped open. GROUP SCREAM:

"AAAAAAAAAHHHHHHHHHHHHHHH!!!!!!!!!!!"

Chapter 5
The Marshmallow Meltdown

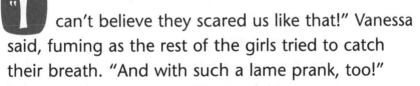

"I can't believe they scared us like that!" Vanessa said, fuming as the rest of the girls tried to catch their breath. "And with such a lame prank, too!"

Still, by taking the girls by surprise and shouting "BOO!" Mike and Jay really *had* scared the stuffing out of them.

"Well, maybe the boys didn't see how much they frightened us," Gwen offered.

"Are you kidding?" O'Ryan asked. "You jumped so high, I thought you were going to hit your head on the ceiling."

"Well, you screamed so loud, I thought you were going to break glass," Reese replied to her twin, coming to the defense of her BFF.

"Stop, girls!" Vanessa interrupted. "That doesn't matter now. What *does* matter is figuring out how we're gonna get the boys back!"

Reese and O'Ryan looked at each other. They both knew that Vanessa was right. BUT both also knew that Vanessa was acting like a bossy know-it-all.

And they didn't like it at *all*.

Reese leaned over and whispered into her twin's ear, "Just because she's one grade older doesn't mean she should be so bossy!"

"I'm with you, sister!" O'Ryan nodded.

"So," Vanessa continued, "what are we going to do now?"

The girls thought for a moment.

Which became two minutes.

Which turned into a solid five.

Then they all just shook their heads. They were out of ideas.

"I think my head would *think* better," Gwen said, "if I had something in my stomach."

"You know what?" Vanessa replied. "That's not a bad idea at all, Gwen!"

"Oh, gee, thanks," Gwen replied, rolling her

eyes. Then she turned to Reese and whispered, "Haven't I been saying that all along?"

"We're losing our mojo, girls," Vanessa went on, sounding like a regular General Groovy-nator. "We need to eat something sugary ASAP to bring up our energy. And if we make these s'mores," she added, grabbing Gwen's bag, "it should help us think better."

"I'd say you're thinking better already!" Yvette commented.

The girls ran into the kitchen to get started.

Since Yvette was the one who loved to cook, she started organizing the ingredients. First, she arranged the box of graham crackers and the two big Hershey bars. Then, she reached for the marshmallows.

"Uh-oh," she said.

"Uh-oh-what?" Vanessa asked.

"Uh-oh-we-don't-got-no-marshmalloooooowwws," Yvette replied.

"What are you talking about?" Gwen said. "I didn't forget to bring marshmallows. We even used them earlier when we made the...Uh-oh!"

They had used up *every* last marshmallow in the bag to make Mike's bunny.

"Well, you guys must have more marshmallows

around here, right?" Yvette asked Reese and O'Ryan.

"Nope," Reese said. "When Dad went on his diet, he created a 'no marshmallows in the house' rule."

"Did the diet work?" Oki asked.

"Nope," O'Ryan replied. "'Cause it just made him eat the marshmallows faster as he was bringing the shopping bag in from the car to the house!"

"Well, what are we going to do?" Vanessa said, putting her hands on her hips.

"Wait a second," Reese said. "Yvette's a great chef. She might be able to whip up s'mores without marshmallows, right?"

"Well," Yvette said, smiling, "I think even *I* would need at least one more ingredient."

O'Ryan went to the cabinet to see what they could offer as a marshmallow substitute.

"If anyone can make marshmallow-less s'mores work, it's Yvette. She's a culinary G-E-E-N-Y-U-S," Gwen spelled out.

"I think you mean G-E-N-I-U-S," Yvette replied.

"I bet you could even make *this* taste good!" O'Ryan laughed, pulling a jar of pickled artichoke hearts out from the cabinet.

"Artichokes!?" Yvette cried, her face scrunching with disgust. "*B*-to the-*L*-to the *ECK*! BLECK! Those are nasty."

"Oh, come on, Yvette," Oki teased. "You're not giving them a chance. I mean, you're going to have to be more open-minded about your ingredients. 'Specially if you want your very own show on the Food Network someday."

"That's right!" Vanessa nodded. "Think of it as a challenge. You'll be our very own *Iron Chef*!"

"Guys," Yvette replied, "I'm sorry, but I can't make *that* taste good. It's way too yucky. I mean, smell these things!"

When Yvette cracked open the jar, all the other girls leaned in to take a sniff of the stink.

And all their mouths curved into cartoon frowns.

"See?" Yvette said. "Told ya. I mean, if I made s'mores with pickled artichoke hearts, it'd be a joke. A gross joke."

When Yvette said that, a lightbulb went off over Vanessa's head.

"*A gross joke!*" Vanessa repeated. "That's it! Who's thinking what I'm thinking?"

The other girls looked at her blankly.

"It would be a great joke to serve pickled artichoke s'mores to a certain prankster we all know," she continued.

All of a sudden, five more lightbulbs went off over Groovy heads.

"Interesting," Yvette nodded.

"So you want to serve icky s'mores to Mike?" Oki asked, making sure she was understanding correctly.

"To Mike and his fellow joker, Jay," Vanessa replied. "Let's get cooking!"

Yvette took the graham crackers and chocolate, and broke them into squares. She placed the chocolate on the crackers. Then she put them in the pan in the toaster oven.

"This will melt the chocolate a little," Yvette explained.

O'Ryan programmed the toaster, and when the

bell dinged a little while later, the girls carefully removed the pan.

"Mmm," Gwen said, closing her eyes, "you *are* a good cook, Yvette."

"Thanks, but once I add the pickled artichokes, you won't be saying that," Yvette replied.

After she placed an artichoke on top of a chocolate-covered cracker, Yvette placed another graham cracker on top of that, finishing off her creation.

She held the artichoke-stuffed s'more up for inspection. "What do you think, girls?"

"If I didn't know better," O'Ryan said, "I'd eat that in a minute."

"Are you kidding?" Gwen said. "It wouldn't take *me* a whole minute to eat it, if it were a real s'more."

Vanessa looked at the s'more very closely.

She examined it from every angle.

She cocked her head to the side.

She narrowed her eyes.

Then she put her index finger to her mouth, tapping it against her lips.

"I think," Vanessa replied, pausing for effect, "it looks perfect!"

"Yeah," said Gwen, "perfectly revolting!"

"Great job, Yvette!" Oki added.

"Now, let's make a whole plate of these sick snacks and head over to Mike's," Vanessa said.

All the girls pitched in to assemble the fake s'mores. And as soon as they'd laid the last pickled artichoke on the chocolaty graham crackers, they were ready to head back on the bunny trail.

Vanessa was in charge again, with the rest of the girls behind her.

And with their tricked-out treats in hand, the Groovies marched over to Mike's house to serve up their pickled prank!

Chapter 6

Special Delivery

"Y ou boys are just better at it than us girls," Vanessa said, handing Mike and Jay the plate of s'mores. "We can't outdo you when it comes to pulling pranks."

"So what are these for?" Mike asked. He eyed the smiling girls and the tray of treats.

"We made them," Oki replied sweetly. "To mark the end of the prank wars."

"Yeah," Vanessa added. "We've come in peace."

"What?" Jay asked.

"Peace," Reese repeated. "P-E-A-C-E."

"I don't get it," Mike said, crossing his arms.

"Here, I'll use it in a sentence," Reese continued. "We hate war, and we want peace."

"All we are saying, is give peace a chance," Yvette sang.

"Now do you get it?" Oki asked.

"Not really," Jay said.

"Well, you guys saw how much you scared us when you snuck up on us before, right?" O'Ryan explained.

The boys smiled and nodded at the memory.

"Gwen jumped so high I thought she was going to leapfrog over Reese," Mike replied.

Gwen didn't find this very amusing. "Not funny, Bunny Lover," she said.

"Anyway," Yvette added, "these delicious s'mores are to show you that we give up. You win."

Mike and Jay looked at each other.

Were they buying it?

Or would they see right through the girls' prank?

"Well," Mike said, a smile forming on his lips. "It's about time you girls realized that we're just better at this stuff than you are."

"Yeah," Jay agreed. "'Cause if you didn't give

up, it'd only get worse for you."

"Wow," Oki said, playing along. "We can't even imagine what other great pranks you might have pulled on us!"

"That's right." Mike nodded. "You don't even have a clue!"

"It's good you're doing things you understand better now—like making snacks for us," Jay said smugly, leaning into the tray of s'mores. "*Mmm*, these look good."

When Gwen thought about Mike and Jay taking big bites of the artichoke s'mores, she could feel herself getting giggly. She could sense the laugh coming on. It was like one of those slow-moving sneezes you could feel at the top of your nose!

"Well," Reese replied. "We just hope you enjoy them and think of us while you eat them!"

"Come on, girls," Vanessa said. "Let's let the boys eat...in *peace*."

"Have a good night, guys!" Reese added happily.

"Good night," Mike said, then closed the door.

It wasn't until the girls got back to the McCloud's that they allowed themselves to look at one another.

Then their full-bellied laughter started raining down in buckets. They laughed harder when they imagined how the boys would look when they ate those icky s'mores.

"Bet Mike would look like this," Gwen said, screwing up her face. She stuck out her tongue and held her stomach.

"Or like this!" Reese said, grabbing at her throat and making gagging noises.

"Or like *this*!" said Yvette, clapping her hands to both sides of her face and bugging out her eyes.

After mimicking the boys, the Groovies ran up to the twins' bedroom and flopped down on their sleeping bags.

In the middle of the sleeping-bag circle, the girls saw a pizza box.

"Thanks for the 'za, Ma," O'Ryan yelled downstairs.

Sure, they'd all eaten dinner, but as Gwen would be the first to say, that was ages ago.

"What should we do now?" Reese asked, grabbing a slice.

"I don't know," Yvette yawned, "but it feels like there are elephants on my eyelids."

"Yeah," Gwen agreed, catching the yawn, and yawning herself. "I'm a little bit tired, too."

And the belly-filling warm pizza wasn't exactly making them want to jump around.

"*I'm* not tired," Oki said. "It's just that my arms, legs, and head are."

"I *know* we swore we'd stay up all night this time," Yvette said. "But I'm not sure I'm going to make it."

It had been a Groovy Goal to stay awake till morning. Since the girls had all accidentally fallen asleep at their last sleepover, they wanted to do better this time.

In fact, they'd made a pact. They'd made a pledge. They'd made a promise.

But their energy was sapping like maple syrup from a tree.

"Okay. I'm making an executive decision," Vanessa said, standing up and putting her hands on her hips.

"I'm calling off the no-sleep part of this sleepover."

"Huh?" Gwen asked, sort of curious. But also sort of too tired to really care.

"If we officially say we're not staying awake all night, we won't have broken our promise if we fall asleep," Vanessa explained. "So on my official say-so, the no-sleep sleepover part of our sleepover is over."

Case closed.

Or so Vanessa thought.

But as Vanessa was making her "official" announcement, O'Ryan and Reese looked at each other. Vanessa was doing EXACTLY the thing they didn't like. She was acting like the boss.

Again!

"Okay, girls," Vanessa said, as bossy as ever. "Let's get the jammies on, the teeth brushed, and the lights out. Five minutes."

O'Ryan and Reese, with that special twin thing going on between them, suddenly knew what to do. O'Ryan walked over to the stereo and turned it on.

Then she turned it up.

Blast-off-level loud!

Letting the music move her, Reese started to dance. As soon as Gwen saw Reese groovin', she got up to join in. The girls bopped back and forth.

They were poetry in motion!

Vanessa stomped over to the radio and turned it off with a hard flick of the switch.

"Um, excuse me?" Vanessa said. "Didn't we just decide that we were going to sleep now?"

O'Ryan crossed her arms. "No," she said, "*WE* didn't just decide that."

"*YOU* decided that," Reese added.

"But we're all tired," Vanessa replied, throwing up her hands.

"That's right," O'Ryan nodded. "But we're also *tired* of you always running the show!"

Vanessa was stunned. "You're kidding, right?"

"Well, honestly?" Oki said. "You *are* kind of bossy."

"Well, I'm sorry you guys think that," Vanessa replied, trying not to sound hurt. "But here's the thing: Taking charge is just what I do. It's who I am, you know?"

"Vanessa," Gwen said, "it's not that we don't want you to be who you are. 'Cause of course we all think you're this great gal—"

"Who's a great leader," Reese added.

"And an awesome soccer player," O'Ryan said.

"But if you think about it," Gwen continued, "everyone here is pretty supreme, too."

"And a lot of us have good ideas and want to have a say in things," Oki added.

Vanessa didn't say anything for a few seconds, but then she nodded. She got it.

"Okay," she finally said. "I promise to try to be more thoughtful about things in the future."

"Thanks," O'Ryan said.

"And I swear I'll listen to whatever you guys have to say—and *then* I'll make the official decision," she joked.

"Hey, I have a great idea!" Yvette said.

"Well, let's hear it!" Gwen shouted.

"Who thinks we should call off the official no-sleep sleepover now and go to bed?"

The girls all laughed, raised their hands, and shouted, "Me! Me! Me! Me!"

And so it was official: The no-sleep part of the sleepover was kaput!

After they took turns brushing their teeth, they washed their faces: Strawberry-scented soap for Reese and Gwen. Pear-smelling scrub for Oki and O'Ryan. Watermelon wash for Yvette and Vanessa.

Then, glammie jammies on, the girls finally got into their sleeping bags.

But before Oki and O'Ryan fell asleep, Oki tapped her best friend.

"Hey," she whispered, "can I tell you a secret?"

"Of course," O'Ryan replied. "What's going on?"

"I'm a little scared," Oki replied.

"You are? About what?" O'Ryan sat up.

"Well, you know how I totally didn't believe in that Ouija dude phantom thingy before?" Oki said.

"Yeah?"

"Well, once it started speaking Japanese, it really freaked me out."

"You mean, 'cause the board knew Nyan's name meant *meow* in English?" O'Ryan asked.

"Uh-huh." Oki nodded.

"Uh-boy," O'Ryan replied. "What's the Japanese word for 'whoops'?"

"Why?"

"'Cause I didn't know you were scared! If I did, I would have reminded you that *you'd told me* what Nyan meant when you first got the cat."

"I told you that? Really? And you remembered?" Oki asked.

"Yeah! He's *your* cat. And *you're my* best friend."

"But still," Oki said, shaking her head, "the pointer moved it to those letters. Not you."

"Sure," O'Ryan replied, "but I was pushing the pointer."

Oki looked at O'Ryan and narrowed her eyes. This sure *did* sound like something her best friend would do.

And Oki also knew O'Ryan would tell her the truth at a moment like this. "Okay, you got me," Oki said, laughing and punching O'Ryan lightly on the arm. "But if you ever try to pull something like that on me again, you are so gonna…" Oki tried to think of a proper punishment. "You are so gonna have to wear my shoes that went out of style last season!"

"No! No! Not that!" O'Ryan laughed. "Anything but that!"

The two girls giggled and lay down in their sleeping bags.

They were totally ready to go to sleep now.

Chapter 7

How Do You Spell G-O-T-C-H-A?

THE BIG SPELLING BEE

"**A**sk me how much I love our slumber parties," Reese said to Gwen in Mrs. Pearlman's classroom on Monday morning.

"As much as I do?" Gwen asked, smiling.

"Well, if you love our sleepovers as much as I love my butterfly collection, and the puppy I'm hoping to get for my next birthday, then you totally do," Reese replied.

"I bet Mike and Jay are so not going to want to show up today with the way we got them back with the artichoke s'mores," Gwen said, as she hung up her jacket in her cubby.

"So they're not here?" Reese asked.

"Not yet!" Gwen replied. "Maybe they'll be no-shows 'cause they're sick to their stomachs."

Gwen and Reese laughed, then did a mini version of their Groovy Girls victory dance.

Oki and O'Ryan were also discussing the weekend's adventures. But since Mike hadn't arrived yet, Oki had decided to sit in his seat.

"Look at me, I'm Mike," Oki said, squirming around.

"No wonder you can't sit still. Must be the artichoke s'mores you ate on Saturday night!" O'Ryan replied, laughing.

"Okay," Mrs. P. said as she walked into the room. "Everyone in his or her own seats, please."

Right behind Mrs. P. came Mike and Jay.

Oki batted her eyelashes at Mike when she stood up, playfully holding his chair out for him. "Thought you could use the help," she said, giggling as she returned to her seat.

"Good morning, class!" Mrs. P. said.

"Good morning, Mrs. Pearlman," everyone

responded in unison.

"I hope you all had a good weekend. And I hope that we're all a little better rested this morning."

The Groovy Girls looked at one another and smiled. Better rested?

As *if*!

But was their second Monday of being tired worth it?

In a word:

YesTotallyAbsolutelyOneHundredPercentNoDoubt.

"So we're going to start off this morning with some spelling exercises to help us prepare for the school-wide bee," Mrs. P. said.

Reese leaned over to Gwen. "With all the spelling we did with that Ouija board, I bet we're gonna R-O-C-K the B-E-E!"

"T-O-T-A-L-L-E-E," Gwen replied, misspelling *totally*.

"When I call on you, please come up to the front of the room," Mrs. P. said. "I'll say a word, and you'll spell it. If you get it right, you get a point. Then, I'll ask you to use the word in a sentence, to show you know the word's meaning. If it's a good sentence, you'll get two more points. And whoever has the most points at the end will win a prize."

"Fun!" O'Ryan said.

"Okay, Reese," Mrs. P. called out. "Please step forward."

Reese smiled at her friends as she walked to the front of the room.

"Your word is *pumpkin*."

"Easy," Reese said. "P-U-M-P-K-I-N. And my sentence is, 'I like to carve pumpkins for Halloween.'"

"Very nice, Reese," Mrs. Pearlman replied. "Three points."

Reese high-fived Gwen as she sat back down.

"Okay, Mike, your turn."

Mike didn't make eye contact with any of the girls as he walked to the front of the room. And suddenly, O'Ryan started to feel a little guilty about playing their last prank on him.

She hoped he wasn't feeling too bad about it.

After all, she and Mike had *sort of* been friends before Saturday night's prank wars. The two of them would even shoot hoops in his driveway together sometimes after school.

"Please spell the word *artichoke*," Mrs. P. said to Mike.

"No way!" Gwen giggled.

"Too F-U-N-N-Y," Reese whispered.

But the look on Mike's face was very serious. "Artichoke," he said. "A-R-T-I-C-H-O-K-E."

"Good," Mrs. P. responded. "And now for your sentence."

"Right," Mike said, and that's when the expression on his face began to change.

And as the girls watched him, they thought something seemed strange. It was the way Mike began to smile.

And then it was what Mike said. "I...*LOVE* artichokes. In fact," he continued, "there's nothing I like better than the salty, delicious taste of an artichoke heart."

A-R-T-I-C-H-O-K-E...
I...LOVE artichokes. In fact, there's nothing I like better than the salty, delicious taste of an artichoke heart.

Wait.

What?

Did Mike just say he loved artichokes???

"Okay, thank you, Mike," Mrs. Pearlman replied.

"Well, actually," Mike continued, "I'm not done. Even better than eating artichokes plain is getting to eat them when they're smothered in chocolate and stuck between two graham crackers. That's when they're called artichoke s'mores."

"Mike," Mrs. Pearlman replied, somewhat puzzled. "That's more than enough."

But Mike still wasn't done. He continued.

"You know, if I had to go to a desert island, the one food I'd take with me would be artichoke s'mores. *Mmm, mmm,* good!"

"Yeah," Jay yelled out. "If only I knew where we could get *some more*!"

Gwen looked at Reese.

Reese looked at Oki.

Oki looked at O'Ryan.

O'Ryan looked at Gwen.

(And if Vanessa and Yvette had been in their class, they'd be looking at each other, too. And they'd be looking just as astonished as the others.)

"No way!" Gwen said.

·"This is un-*bee*-lievable," Reese replied, shaking her head.

Oki quickly scribbled a note to O'Ryan and tossed it to her.

Dear O'Ryan,
Can it really be true? Do you think the boys really like artichokes? Did our prank go over as flat as a popped balloon?
Yours in stun-dom,
Oki

O'Ryan shook her head. She couldn't believe it, either. Unless the boys were pranking.

And that's when Mike caught O'Ryan's eye as he walked back to his desk. He nodded at her.

And it was a nice nod.

It was a nod from one great prankster to another.

It was a nod, but more like a wink.

And suddenly O'Ryan got it.

She quickly wrote a note back to Oki, and tossed it to her.

Dear Oki,

Don't know if the boys really like artichokes, OR if this is just another one of their pranks. Maybe we're evenly matched after all. Either way, can't wait till our next sleepover!

Yours in Grooviness,
O'Ryan